Birth of
THE MONKEY KING

Based on *Journey to the West*
by Wu Cheng'en

New Translation by Li Chaoyuan
Illustrations by Lu Xinsen & Yan Dingxian

INTRODUCTION

According to legend, at the beginning of time the universe consisted only of a darkness known as chaos. After 5,400 years, light matter soared upward and formed the sun, the moon, and the stars in the sky.

Then 5,400 years later, heavy matter sank to form water, fire, mountains, rocks, and soil on the earth.

After another 5,400 years, all living creatures came to be.

The world divided into four continents: the Eastern, the Western, the Southern, and the Northern.

On the Eastern Continent stood a mountain of flowers and fruit, on top of which lay an immortal rock. After the sky separated from the earth, the sun and moon nourished the rock daily until it became divine and acquired supernatural powers, which eventually created a considerable stir in Heaven.

More than 500 years later, monks from the Southern Continent were sent to get Buddhist sutras from the Western Continent, so that people on their home continent could be relieved of pain and suffering.

Their pilgrimage did not succeed until they endured eighty-one trials with the help of the disciples, including our irrepressible hero the Monkey King.

On an island in the Kingdom of Aolai on the Eastern Continent was Flowers and Fruit Mountain. On top of this mountain was a mystical rock.

Ever since the heavens were divided from the earth, the rock had absorbed their essence, and the sun and moon nourished the rock until it became divine and acquired supernatural powers. One day, it burst open and produced a stone monkey.

Right away, the monkey learned to climb and run, and quickly mastered climbing trees and swinging between branches. He enjoyed a happy life on the mountain, drinking from streams, picking flowers, and eating fruit.

Before long, the stone monkey became friends with other monkeys. One hot summer day while the monkeys were playing in a mountain stream, they discovered a magnificent waterfall arching down from a cliff like a rainbow.

An old monkey said, "If anyone can pass through the waterfall and return unharmed, we shall make him our king."

The old monkey called out three times, but no one dared to try.

Suddenly, the stone monkey jumped out of the crowd and volunteered. "I'll go in!" he exclaimed. He closed his eyes, crouched, and sprang through the waterfall.

Once he was inside the waterfall, he opened his eyes to find himself in a spacious cave. Straight ahead of him was an iron bridge. A stone tablet in the middle of it was engraved with the words,

WATER-CURTAIN CAVE

ON THE BLESSED

FLOWERS AND FRUIT MOUNTAIN

The stone monkey leaped onto the bridge and walked further inside. Looking around, he was delighted to find that the cave was like a mansion, completely furnished with stone benches and beds, as well as stone pans, pots, stoves, and bowls.

"How wonderful!" he said to himself. "This is a perfect, homey place. We can all move in here to shelter from the heat and rain and Heaven's erratic temper."

Hurrying back to the entrance, the stone monkey crouched again and jumped back out through the water. He described everything he saw in the cave to the other monkeys. They were so excited that they wanted to go with him to see it with their own eyes.

"Follow me, everyone!" said the stone monkey. The monkeys followed, jumping through the water curtain into the cave.

The group bounded after him across the bridge and entered the residence. They were curious about everything and quarreled over the pots, bowls, stove, and beds.

As agreed, the monkeys crowned the stone monkey their king. They brought out delicious wine and fresh fruit for a great celebration.

From then on, the stone monkey was called the "Monkey King."

The Monkey King appointed some apes, monkeys, and macaques to ministerial positions. The monkeys enjoyed their lives on Flowers and Fruit Mountain during the day and returned to Water-Curtain Cave at night. They indulged in fresh fruit, mountain streams, and fine wine. Instead of competing with birds and beasts as before, they had the mountain to themselves and were happy.

Thus the Monkey King lived a carefree life for three to five hundred years. One day, he suddenly felt sad and began to weep. When the monkeys asked why, he said, "Although I have a happy life now, I know that someday I will grow old and die."

Upon hearing this, the monkeys also felt sad and began to weep.

"I now see why your Majesty is sad," said an old monkey emerging from the group. "In this world, only immortals and Buddhas have eternal life. You can go and learn from them if you wish."

"Where?" the Monkey King asked.

"In ancient caves on those divine mountains," answered the old monkey.

Delighted, the Monkey King immediately ordered the monkeys to cut down trees to make him a raft, find some sturdy bamboo for long poles, and gather dried fruit for his journey. He was eager to travel to the ends of the earth to find immortals and Buddhas and learn from them the secret of eternal life.

The next day, the monkeys prepared a farewell feast for their king. They gathered all kinds of fruit and flowers, neatly set up stone stools and tables, and arranged delicious wine and food on them. The Monkey King sat on the throne, while the other monkeys took turns toasting their king and offering him fruit and flowers. They ate and drank to their hearts' content.

Early the next morning, the Monkey King jumped on the raft alone, pushed off with the pole, and headed out into the ocean. The monkeys on the shore wept and bade him farewell.

With the help of the wind and waves, the Monkey King traveled a long distance on his raft and lost track of time. One day, he saw land in the distance. He had come to the Southern Continent.

He landed on the shore and saw people fishing, hunting wild geese, digging clams, and mining salt. Mischievous by nature, Monkey approached them and made funny faces to scare the people. They dropped their baskets and nets and ran away as fast as their legs could carry them.

Monkey caught a slow man, took his clothes, and put them on to look like a human before venturing into busy areas.

While walking the many streets and alleys, the Monkey King learned human manners and speech. In order to find the immortals and Buddhas, he spent eight or nine years visiting numerous cities and towns.

One day, Monkey arrived at the Western Ocean. Thinking that the immortals must be on the other side of the ocean, he built another raft and traveled to the Western Continent.

He came ashore and saw a beautiful mountain. As he began climbing, he heard singing and the sound of wood chopping. When the Monkey King listened closely, the music sounded celestial and divine, so he rushed toward the voice to find its source and called out, "Hey, immortal!"

"How could I be an immortal?" the man replied. "I'm just a poor woodcutter, with very little food or clothing."

"But I do know an immortal around here," said the woodcutter, pointing. "That mountain is called Heart and Soul Mountain. There, in the Cave of Tilted Moon and Three Stars lives an immortal called Master Puti. It's not far. Follow this path seven or eight miles south and you'll be there."

Monkey followed the woodcutter's directions and found a cave before long. The entrance was closed. He looked around and found a stone tablet inscribed with huge characters

CAVE OF TITLED MOON AND THREE STARS

ON HEART AND SOUL MOUNTAIN

The Monkey King rejoiced that he had finally found the place. But he was so awed that he dared not knock on the door and nervously climbed a tree to eat its nuts.

In a moment, the door opened, and a young man came out. Monkey jumped down from the tree and greeted him.

"Are you here for our Master?" the young man asked with a smile.

Monkey said yes.

"Our master was about to begin his lecture when he suddenly asked me to go out and welcome a visitor. Come with me."

Monkey quickly straightened his clothes and followed the young man into the cave. Deep in the cave they passed row after row of pavilions and palaces and countless secluded rooms.

They arrived at the foot of a jade dais to find Master Puti sitting atop it, flanked by thirty subordinate immortals standing on each side.

The Monkey King immediately bowed down and continued kowtowing. "Master! Master!" he said, "I have traveled across oceans and long distances and searched for more than ten years to find you here. Please take me in as your student."

"Where do you live?" asked the Master. "What is your family name? What are you called?"

"I am from the Water-Curtain Cave on Flowers and Fruit Mountain in the Kingdom of Aolai on the Eastern Continent," replied the Monkey King. "I don't have a name. I don't have parents either. I was born from a rock. May I ask you, Master, to give me a name?"

"Get up and walk for me," said the Master. "Let me have a look." Monkey jumped up and walked around. The Master chuckled. "Well, you are not handsome. You look like a monkey who eats nuts from pine cones. Your surname will be Sun, which can mean grandson or descendant, but also sounds like our word for monkey. As for your given name, I have special ones for my students. I give you the name 'Wukong' to show my hope for your spiritual journey. How do you like it?"

The Monkey King was thrilled and thanked the Master.

Monkey then went outside and met his fellow students. From the next day on, he studied speech and etiquette with them, discussed scripture, practiced calligraphy, and burned incense every day.

In his spare time, the Monkey King performed all kinds of chores such as sweeping the yard, weeding the garden, pruning the trees and flowers, gathering firewood, and fetching water. He was always enthusiastic to help.

Monkey also practiced kung fu with his fellow students. They all demonstrated great skill with various weapons, from swords and fighting knives to spears and quarterstaffs. But Wukong was the best of all. His bladework could eclipse the sun and the moon, and his sword flashed like a meteor streaking across the sky.

Six or seven years passed in a flash. One day during a lecture by the Master, Wukong smiled and even started wiggling his ears and scratching his cheeks.

"Why can't you focus on listening to me?" scolded the Master.

"I became too excited by the wonderful ideas in your lecture, Master," replied Monkey. "Please forgive me."

"How long have you been here?" asked the Master.

"I can't say for sure," answered Wukong. "The only thing I remember is that I have enjoyed ripe peaches from the trees on the mountain seven times."

"That means you have been here seven years," said the Master. "What do you want to learn from me?"

"Your teachings, Master," Monkey answered.

"I can teach you to summon immortals and do divination so that you can seek good fortune and avoid evil," said the Master.

"No," said Wukong. "Learning this won't give me eternal life."

"Then I'll teach you to be quiet and meditate?"

Again Monkey refused. "No, no. That won't make me immortal either."

The Master suggested several other subjects, but Monkey rejected all of them. The Master jumped off the dais and scolded him. "Nothing is good enough for you, is it? What on earth do you want?" He then hit Wukong on the head with a ruler three times, walked away with his hands behind his back, and shut the center door, leaving everyone behind.

The frightened students criticized Wukong. "What a rude Monkey! What is wrong with you? The Master offered you all those subjects. Why not learn them? Yet you refused and disrespected him!"

They all blamed him, but Monkey smirked because he had learned something important from the Master's reactions.

At midnight when everyone else was asleep, Monkey rose quietly, dressed, and walked down the path to the back door. He was quite pleased to find the door open.

Monkey crept in and proceeded to the Master's bed, where he found him asleep on his right side, with one hand under his cheek. Not daring to disturb the Master, Wukong knelt by the bed.

Soon, the Master awoke and saw him. He sat up and said, "What are you doing here, Monkey?"

Wukong said, "Master, you hit me with a ruler three times, which meant you wanted me to come and see you at the third watch of the night hours. You walked away toward your room with your hands behind your back and closed the central door, which meant you wanted me to come to you using the back door. So here I am, your disciple, waiting for you to teach me the secret of eternal life."

Delighted with the explanation, the Master thought, "How smart this Monkey is to decode my message! He truly must have been nourished by heaven and earth." He then asked Wukong to come close and whispered the secret of eternal life into his ear.

Monkey immediately learned the magical instructions by heart and thanked the Master. When he returned to his room, the other students were still sound asleep, and nobody knew he had received secret enlightenment.

From then on, Wukong practiced his student work during the day and at night practiced the wonderful secrets the Master taught him, including the ancient technique of controlling his breath. After three years, Monkey had learned the seventy-two transformations from his Master.

The Master also taught him the cloud-somersault. In just one somersault, he could travel more than 108,000 miles.

One fine day in early summer, the students sat talking under a pine tree. "Have you learned the seventy-two transformations from the Master?" his fellow students asked Wukong.

"I won't hide it from you, Brothers," Monkey said with pride. "It's true. I have learned them all."

"Then show us what you can do," the others demanded.

"All right, let me start with a cloud-somersault," Monkey said grandly. He recited the spell and jumped up. In a split second, he rose high in the sky on a cloud and disappeared with a somersault.

In the blink of an eye, he returned by cloud-somersault and stepped off. With loud applause, the others asked him to transform into a pine tree.

Wukong recited the spell and changed into a tall pine tree.

While the others were still admiring the pine tree, Monkey rose, turned into an elegant crane, landed on the ground, and nodded to them.

His show won laughter and applause from everyone.

Alarmed by the noise, the Master came out and asked, "Who is making this noise here?"

The students all straightened their clothes and knelt. "Wukong was showing us his transformations, and we were cheering for him," they admitted. "Our loud noise disturbed you, Master. Please forgive us."

The Master then asked the others to leave and said to Wukong, "If you stay here and keep showing off your skills, I'm afraid it will cause great trouble. You must go back where you came from."

Monkey realized his mistake at once. With tears in his eyes, he said, "Master, please forgive me. I cannot leave without repaying the debt I owe for your kindness."

"What debt?" said the Master. "The greatest kindness I could ask for is that you not get into trouble and never involve me. That is all the thanks I need."

Seeing that the Master's mind was made up, Wukong bade everyone farewell.

"Wherever you go, you are bound to create trouble," the Master said with a sigh. "No matter what problems you get into in the future, never tell anyone that you were my student. If you say even half a word about it, I will know and I will punish you so thoroughly you will not be able to sit down for the rest of your life."

After saying goodbye to the Master, Wukong thought about how long ago he had left Flowers and Fruit Mountain—twenty years! He had no idea how his tribe was doing and longed to see them. Reciting the spell for a cloud-somersault, he headed straight back to the mountain.

In less than an hour, he arrived. Walking along the road and seeing the familiar scenery again filled him with excitement.

"Hey everyone, I'm back!" he called out.

From underneath the cliff, from behind trees and boulders and ridges, from fields of grasses and flowers, thousands of monkeys old and young jumped out and surrounded their king with great joy.

"Your Majesty, why were you away so long?" asked one monkey. "Recently, a monster tried to take over Water-Curtain Cave. We managed to guard, risking our lives, but he robbed us of our possessions and kidnapped our children. If you had not returned, we and the cave would soon belong to him."

The Monkey King was enraged. "What demon would dare to be so barbaric?"

The monkeys said, "The Demon King of Chaos, who lives in the north."

The Monkey King comforted his subjects. "Don't be afraid. I will go find him and take revenge." He then launched a cloud, sped northward with a somersault, and soon arrived at a steep mountain. At the foot of the mountain he saw a dirty cave.

Several small demons near the cave entrance tried to flee at the sight of the Monkey King.

"Freeze!" he called out. "Go tell your king that the King of Water-Curtain Cave on Flowers and Fruit Mountain is here. I will make him pay for bullying my children and grandchildren."

The little demons hurried into the cave and reported to their king, "Your Majesty, bad news! Outside there is a monkey who calls himself the King of Water-Curtain Cave on Flowers and Fruit Mountain. He said he wants you to pay for what you did to his subjects."

The Demon King laughed. "The monkeys always said they had a king who was on pilgrimage. He must be back. What does he look like? What kind of weapons does he have?"

"He looks like an ordinary monkey," replied a small demon. "He doesn't look like a Buddhist or Taoist. He has no weapons, but he is very loud."

The Demon King ordered the smaller demons to bring him armor and weapons. The small demons hurried to obey. The Monster King put his armor on, took up his sword, and went outside with the small demons.

He burst into laughter upon seeing Wukong. "Look at you! How small you are, and you have no weapons! I'm so much bigger than you that if I use my broadsword in our fight, people will make fun of me. To be fair, let us both use our fists."

"Good man," said the Monkey King. "Let's get started!"

The punching and kicking began.

The Demon King's long hands and feet proved clumsy, and he needed room to fight. The Monkey King was small and nimble and able to dart in close to his opponent to jab him in vital areas.

The Demon King was soon badly hurt and fell onto his back.

Seeing their king losing the upper hand, a crowd of small demons circled the Monkey King and ran toward him from all sides. Undismayed, Wukong jumped up out of the circle and escaped the crowd, confusing the small demons and leaving them to crash into each other at the center and fight.

The Demon King got back to his feet, picked up his sword, and slashed at the Monkey King. Wukong dodged. The Demon King swung his blade again and again. He missed each time, only to hear the Monkey King laughing behind him.

Infuriated, the Demon King turned around and swung the sword with even greater force.

Seeing how fierce his opponent was, Wukong cast a spell. He plucked a handful of his own hairs, chewed them into pieces, spat them into the air, and shouted, "Change!"

Instantly two or three hundred little copies of the Monkey King encircled the Demon King.

It turned out that this spell was part of the magic that Wukong had learned. He could transform any of his 84,000 hairs from the root to fight for him. Like the Monkey King, the little monkey copies were smart and flexible enough to avoid any weapons attack. The little monkeys squeezed and tugged the Demon King, wrenching at his feet until they knocked him to the ground.

The Monkey King quickly seized the Demon King's sword, moved the small monkeys aside, and killed his opponent. He then led the little copies into the cave and killed all the smaller demons.

Wukong shook himself, put all the little monkeys back on his body, and rescued the monkey children who had been kidnapped from Water-Curtain Cave. He recovered the possessions stolen by the Demon King, set the cave on fire, and watched it burn to ashes. Taking the freed monkeys and possessions with him in a cloud-somersault, the Monkey King returned to Flowers and Fruit Mountain.

The monkeys celebrated the reunion and their king's victory with a feast of fruit and wine.

Wukong told them stories about learning from a Master and about defeating the Demon King.

The monkeys showered him with congratulations and said with delight, "Now that our king has the surname Sun, we will all go by the last name Sun."

After defeating the Demon King of Chaos and claiming his sword, the Monkey King realized the importance of martial arts. He practiced every day and taught the other monkeys to make spears and quarterstaffs out of bamboo and swords out of wood. He also taught them to raise flags and banners, use whistles, patrol their territory, charge and retreat as an army, and pitch camps. His monkeys practiced diligently.

However, Wukong soon realized that simple bamboo and wood weapons would not be enough in a real battle against monsters, beasts, or demons.

"We need proper weapons," he said to the monkeys.

"There is a proud kingdom to the east," said an old monkey. "They have a large army, so they must also have many weapons."

Liking the idea, the Monkey King said, "All of you practice here. I'll go get us weapons." Using a cloud-somersault, he quickly reached the capital. Blowing on the ground, he created a sandstorm that turned day into night. Everyone in the city panicked and stayed indoors.

The Monkey King used the cloud as a ram to break into the armory, where he found a wealth of excellent weapons. Needing help, he again plucked some hairs, chewed them, and spat out thousands of little monkeys to help him steal and carry away the weapons.

The Monkey King loaded the helper monkeys and the captured weapons onto a cloud and took them home by somersault. Upon arrival, he had the little monkeys pile up the weapons. He reclaimed his hairs, and his magical helpers disappeared, then the Monkey King called his subjects. The monkeys rushed to the pile and grabbed lances, fighting knives, swords, bows, and crossbows, shouting and playing all day.

The next day, the Monkey King summoned all the monkeys—more than 47,000!

All beasts and monsters on the mountain were alarmed by this. They came to bow to the Monkey King and give him gifts, like golden drums, colorful flags, and armor.

Flowers and Fruit Mountain became busier than ever before. The monkey army diligently trained in martial arts.

Who knew what trouble would come?

All books in our The Irrepressible Monkey King series are based on the Chinese novel *Journey to the West*. Written in the 1500s during the Ming Dynasty by Wu Cheng'en, *Journey to the West* is one of the Four Great Classical Novels of Chinese literature. The story mixes myths and folklore with historical events from the 7th century. There are a few well-known translations into English, some of which are condensed, while others are complete. This book is a new translation into English from an abridged Chinese-language version of *Journey to the West*.

The original text of this work was written in Chinese. The translator, editor, and publisher have made every effort to ensure that the English-language version is as accurate as possible and in keeping with the artistic intent of the author. Because this work reflects a different culture, some of the ideas and attitudes may be unfamiliar to the English-language audience.